Sea Riders

Narissa's Big Race

by Ella Gray

Illustrated by
Tina Frankenstein-Börlin

SCHOLASTIC INC.

Chapter One

"Eat up, Narissa," said her mom. "It's your big day. You can't possibly go all the way to Pearl Reef without any breakfast!"

Narissa made a big effort to nibble at her seaweed pancake. She usually loved it, but today she was too nervous. "I'm trying, Mom, I really am," she replied. "I'm just not hungry."

"*I'll* eat it for you!" chirped Crest, reaching out to grab Narissa's scallop-shell plate.

"No, you won't!" Narissa laughed, and snatched it back from her younger brother. His playful grin made her relax for a minute, and she managed to swallow a few more mouthfuls. "There. It's gone!"

"Well done," said her mom. "Now, you'd better finish getting ready."

Narissa nodded. She looked up at the entrance to their cozy underwater cave. The sunlight was glancing through the waves high above, already lighting up the sea fans that drifted to and fro in the doorway, and glinting off the pinks and creams of the cockleshells that hung on the walls. She'd better hurry up, or she'd be late.

She climbed down from the big gray-blue table, a slab of rock sculpted by the sea in the center of the cave, and swam lightly to her own little cavern. Inside, her pet lantern fish flitted around, filling the room with twinkling light. Narissa went to a cubbyhole in one corner where she kept her clothes, and picked out her favorite outfit. It was made of tiny blue-green shells strung together with sea twine, and decorated with fish scales that glittered when they caught the light. She had inherited it from her grandmother, one of the most famous sea nymph clothing designers in the district, and Narissa was proud to wear it—but she would be even prouder if she managed to exchange it for a Sea Rider's uniform . . .

"Hurry up, Narissa!" floated her mom's voice through the cave.

"Coming!"

Narissa shrugged off her seaweed nightie, and slipped into the lovely shell outfit. She imagined her grandmother smiling at her. *Save this for your most special days*, she'd told Narissa. *And when you wear it, think of me, and believe that your dreams can come true.*

Well, days didn't come much more special than this one. Narissa could hardly believe it had arrived at last. After months of tests, she'd been chosen to represent her district at the Sea Rider trials, and they began today in the great city of Pearl Reef. If she was selected, it really would be a dream come true—she would become a Sea Rider, one of the elite sea horse riders that patrolled the waves of Oceana, keeping it safe.

Narissa swam to the cubbyhole where she kept her jewelry on an empty starfish shell, and picked out a pretty coral necklace to match her outfit. Then she tied back her long, red hair, took her bag down from its shelf, and slung it over her shoulder. She took a deep breath. She was ready.

"You look lovely," her mom told her as she swam out into the main cave again. "I know you'll do really well, sweetheart."

"Of course she will!" said her dad, swimming in through the entrance. "Narissa's the best rider in the district."

"I've never ridden a sea horse, though," said Narissa nervously.

"Of course you haven't," said her dad. "But none of the other candidates will have, either. And you've had plenty of practice on Silver. You'll be fine."

Silver was the family dolphin, and Narissa had been riding him for as long as she could remember. She smiled. "Thanks, Dad. I'll do my best."

"And that's all that matters, sweetheart." Narissa's mom was trying not to sound too anxious, and Narissa understood why. She, too, had once dreamed of becoming a Sea Rider, but she'd been injured just before her trials, twisting her ankle on a sharp piece of coral. There were no second chances, so she'd never qualified. Instead, she'd become a nurse, caring for sick or injured sea nymphs near their home.

"Silver's ready for you, Narissa," her dad told her. "He's just outside."

"Are you sure you don't want us to come with you?" her mom asked, swimming over to her and putting an arm around her shoulders.

Narissa shook her head. "I want to use the journey as a last practice run. And anyway, I'll be way too nervous to talk to anyone."

Crest gave a snort of laughter and a stream of tiny bubbles floated out of his nose. "You'll never be too nervous to talk, Sis!"

Narissa grinned and blew him a kiss. He stuck his tongue out in return, making her giggle. She could always rely on Crest to keep things fun.

"Okay, well, you'd better get going," said her mom. "Good luck!"

Narissa hugged both her parents. Then they all followed her to the entrance of their underwater cave. Silver was swimming in lazy circles just outside, and Narissa whistled. He came over at once, greeting her with his high-pitched squeal, and she mounted him, settling herself behind the big fin on the top of his back.

"Off we go, Silver!" she cried, and gave him a nudge with her heels.

Silver squealed again, and turned around in a swirl of bubbles. Then, with a final wave to her family, Narissa was on her way.

Pearl Reef was over an hour away, a magnificent

underwater city at the end of a long, winding ridge that began not far from Narissa's district. She steered Silver toward the ridge then rode along at the base of it, with the towering silvery rocks to her left. Hermit crabs and lobsters peered out from its cracks, and brightly colored fish darted around the billowing red and purple seaweed that grew up its sides. This was a well-used waterway, so she passed plenty of other sea nymphs on their dolphins, heading out on visits or to harvest the shells that lined the sea floor.

Narissa called out greetings to the nymphs she knew, then concentrated on her riding. Silver was a wise old dolphin now, but he had shown her a trick or two in his time. Sometimes, if she rode carelessly, he'd flip himself upside down and throw her off! Then she had to scold him and make sure she got back on again in a hurry so she didn't lose her nerve.

Today she sat very upright, trying to imagine

10

what it would be like to ride a sea horse. It would be much, much harder than riding a dolphin—Silver's back was broad and comfortable, and he usually swam in a nice flat position that made it easy to stay on. But sea horses' backs were much narrower, with spines all the way down, and you had to learn to ride at an angle because they held themselves more upright than a dolphin ever would. And everyone knew that you had to work very hard to gain a sea horse's respect. That was why they were only ever ridden by Sea Riders, and the trainees at the Sea Riders Academy.

Silver seemed to know that Narissa had her mind on other things today. He swam forward calmly, ignoring her as she tried out different positions, shifted her weight this way and that, leaned forward and then leaned back, or tugged at his fin. Some other sea nymphs passing in the opposite direction gave her some very funny looks, but Narissa hardly noticed.

Then came something she *did* notice. She gripped Silver's fin a little tighter. Actual sea horses! Two of them, with Sea Riders on their backs. Narissa held her breath as they came closer. The sea horses swam forward powerfully, their necks arched and their chests puffed out. Everything else on the highway made way for them—dolphins and sea nymphs, cuttlefish and squid, schools of tiny glittering fish. Narissa felt overcome with awe as she and Silver skirted past them. The Sea Riders stared straight ahead, as though they were completely focused on the task that lay before them. Narissa wondered where they were going. Were they on their way to banish some pirate fish, or perhaps rescue a trapped kelp urchin? She longed to know.

Silver bobbed up and down slightly on the wave that the sea horses left behind them. Narissa rose and fell with his movement, staring back after them. She could hardly believe that soon she would be riding a sea horse, too—even if it was only for the trials. She hugged Silver's fin at the thought of it, then realized she was just sitting without really riding at all. This wouldn't do.

"Come on, Silver," she cried, nudging him forward. "We'll never reach Pearl Reef at this rate!"

Chapter Two

THE WATERWAY GREW busier and busier as they approached the city. Huge schools of red snappers shifted this way and that; seals and huge narwhals sometimes blocked the way entirely, and Narissa had to navigate around them. She started to buzz with excitement as she followed the signs through the alleys and channels to the Sea Rider Academy.

Finally, the city came into view, its golden stone

buildings shifting to brilliant green and turquoise as the sun glanced down through the blue water. Some of its towers and spires glistened white, built in the beautiful marble that was found in the seabed quarries nearby, and in between the buildings rose the waving reds, greens, and yellows of people's anemone gardens. Narissa guided Silver onward, around the city walls, dodging the messenger eels that slithered like quicksilver around everyone else.

At last the Sea Rider Academy came into view, its towering walls jutting out into the ocean. The sea was churning around the entrance as dolphins and porpoises flipped to and fro, their anxious-looking sea nymphs trying to find the right way in. Narissa could see some guards at the massive stone gateway, and waited her turn. At last she was close enough to hear what she was supposed to do.

"Sea Rider candidates. Please leave your dolphins and other creatures in the resting area to the left," shouted one of the guards. "Pass through it to enter the Academy."

Narissa guided Silver around to the left and found a smaller gateway, through which other sea nymphs and their mounts were passing one by one. They went in and found a courtyard lined with purple sea anemones, their fronds waving gently in the cool, dim water. Other dolphins were already there, resting after their journeys. Narissa slipped down from Silver and patted his neck.

"See you later, Silver," she whispered.

She started to swim toward the next doorway when an enormous whale barged in through the gateway, screeching for everyone else to get out of the way. Narissa turned and stared. There were two sea nymphs riding him: a beautiful girl about Narissa's age, with flowing blonde hair and blue eyes, and a woman who looked very much like her, but older—clearly the girl's mother. Both were wearing dresses made of the finest weave, rare sea grass intertwined with threads of silver sea silk, and necklaces that flashed with precious jewels.

"Get down, Tempestua!" ordered the woman. Her beautiful face was stern and hard. "I'll send Bravura to pick you up at the end of the day."

The girl slid down and smoothed back her long hair. The whale turned around in a big swooshing circle, almost hitting one of the others with his tail, while the woman's silver-blonde hair streamed out behind her.

"And remember what I said," she shouted over her shoulder as Bravura headed to the gateway. "Don't let us down!"

There was something so threatening about the way she said this it made Narissa shiver.

Then the massive whale plunged outside, leaving an explosion of bubbles behind him. Narissa spluttered. It was very bad manners for a sea creature to create so much spray. Silver would never behave like that! For a moment, she couldn't even see the doorway she was supposed to be going through. Then the bubbles cleared, and she headed for it again, and reached it at the same time as Tempestua.

Narissa felt a bit sorry for her for having such a bossy mom and rude family whale. "Hi, I'm Narissa," she said. "I guess you're taking part in the trials, too?"

"I'd say that's pretty obvious," snapped Tempestua.

Narissa's face flushed. "Well, I was only . . ." she began, but Tempestua had already turned her back and was heading through the doorway. Narissa's mouth dropped open. The girl was just as bad as her mom—there was no point feeling sorry for her at all.

But as soon as she passed through the door, she forgot about all about Tempestua. She entered a beautiful chamber built of white sea marble, where thousands of lantern fish swam just below the ceiling, lighting the whole chamber so that the marble twinkled and shone. Two Sea Riders appeared, a man and a woman, gliding toward her in their close-fitting mother-of-pearl-colored uniforms. Their bodies were athletic and muscular, but not only that—they seemed to exude wisdom, as though they knew all the secrets of the ocean. Narissa gazed at them, dumbstruck.

"Female candidates to the right, please," called one of the Sea Riders, her voice firm and clear. "Boys to the left. You will all find a uniform of the right size waiting for you."

A uniform! Narissa's heart started to pound. She swam eagerly into the next chamber and there, sure enough, lay rows of suits—not in the elegant mother-of-pearl color that the Sea Riders wore, but a simpler design of turquoise and silver-gray. Other girls were already in there, grinning at each other nervously and swapping names as they changed out of their own clothes. Narissa swam to one corner where the suits looked her size, and began to slip out of her grandmother's special outfit. There were cubbyholes in the rock above each suit where candidates could store their own things, and Narissa had soon wriggled into the neat Sea Rider outfit.

"It fits you perfectly," said a shy voice next to her.

Narissa turned to see a thin, smiling girl close by. She, too, had already changed, and the silver-gray of the uniform looked pretty against her dark hair.

"Thanks," said Narissa, smiling back at her. "You look really good, too. What's your name?"

"Coral," said the girl. "What"s yours?"

"Narissa." She ran her hand down the smooth, silky material of the uniform. She'd never felt anything like it before. "Which district are you from?"

Coral said that she came from far to the east, where there was a reef with lots of dangerous swirling currents and jagged rocks. "Sea creatures are always getting into trouble there," she explained. "That's why I want to become a Sea Rider if I can—so I can help to rescue them."

Narissa was impressed. Coral seemed sweet. "Well, I hope you get through," she said warmly, and really meant it.

"I hope you do, too," said Coral. She gave a little sigh. "I don't think it's going to be easy for any of us."

They turned as a Sea Rider entered the room. "When you're ready, follow me into the arena," she said.

Narissa and Coral swam after her down a corridor lined with pearly razor shells, then turned a corner and passed through a fine curtain of shimmering sea silk. Narissa stared around her, amazed. They were in the huge arena, with its tiered stands of gleaming marble and giant seaweed-covered walls. The boys were already there, lined up in orderly rows in their new uniforms, and right in the center stood a tall, imposing sea nymph, her white hair reaching down beyond her waist. She wore a cloak of the rarest blue seaweed, which

grew only in treacherous crevices. Narissa knew that only Sea Riders were brave enough to find it. The cloak was interwoven with zebra shells, and the sea nymph held a heavy staff topped with a beautiful jewel-encrusted conch.

The girls filed in and formed three rows beside the boys, then stood still as the sea nymph began to speak.

"Welcome to the Sea Rider Academy. I am Neptuna," announced the nymph. "I am the leader of the Sea Riders, and the head of the Academy. Nothing happens here without my consent, and I expect obedience from candidates at all times."

She raised her staff, and its jewels flashed like a warning through the water.

"You have all done very well to have come this far," Neptuna continued. "For that, I congratulate you. But we can only offer places to the truly exceptional. For this reason, many of you will suffer disappointment. At the end of today's trials, there will be only four of you left."

A gasp went up among the candidates.

"That's right," said Neptuna, her blue eyes roving over the candidates. "Just four. So make sure you try your very hardest. There will be no second chances."

Narissa's heart was beating fast. Only four places! She had no idea there would be so few. She'd thought there might be perhaps ten. She sneaked a glance at her rivals. The rows of faces looked glum; everyone was thinking the same thing. There must be at least a hundred candidates. So many of them would have to go home and tell their families they had failed. The competition was going to be even tougher than Narissa had imagined . . .

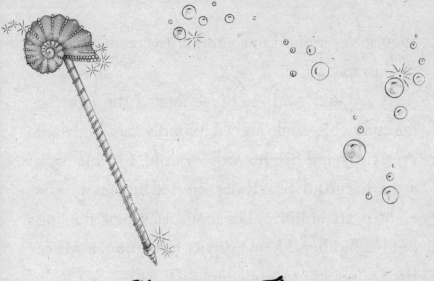

Chapter Three

With a flourish of her staff, Neptuna ordered the trials to begin. In one corner of the arena, the green-gold seaweed walls started to sway and shimmer with a pearly light. Narissa held her breath. She glanced over at Neptuna, who was holding her staff up high, its jeweled conch shell now sending brilliant sparkles of color through the water. She looked back at the walls and saw that the fronds were starting to part, entwining themselves around one another to create a majestic entrance.

A red and gold sea horse floated through the entrance, his neck arched proudly, his big dark eyes clear and bright with wisdom. On his back sat a beautiful Sea Rider dressed in her mother-of-pearl uniform, her long black hair flowing out behind her. Then, in strict formation, a whole herd of sea horses glided in, each with a Sea Rider swimming at their side, their fins sending silver-blue waves rippling around the arena.

A murmur rippled among the candidates, and Narissa felt dizzy with excitement. She'd never been so close to so many sea horses before. Their colors glistened like gems—deep purple-blue, aquamarine and silver, rich coral orange, and stunning scarlet; the crests on their heads shimmered as they circled the arena, each with their name woven with tiny strands of golden sea twine. Their graceful movement seemed effortless, as though the sea itself was at their command.

"Candidates!" boomed Neptuna as the last of the sea horses swam to a halt in front of her. "Your first challenge awaits you. None of you have ridden a sea horse before, so we must see which of you have enough natural talent to take you to the next stage. You will each ride one now. What I will ask you to do may sound easy, but believe me, many will fail."

Narissa gazed at the glistening rows of sea horses. She couldn't believe they were actually going to ride one right away. Then, as Neptuna paused, she caught sight of a sea horse that seemed different from all the others. He was big and powerful, black all over, and his crest had a silvery sheen. Narissa caught his eye, and her heart skipped a beat. He was gorgeous.

"You must each choose a sea horse and mount it," continued Neptuna. "Then ride around the arena in single file so I may see you clearly. Please do not attempt anything beyond your ability. To show off at this stage would be very foolish. Now, choose your horses."

Narissa swam quickly toward the beautiful black sea horse. But just as she drew near, something shoved her elbow, sending her off-balance.

"Hey!" she exclaimed.

But it was too late. The "something" had long golden hair and was already scrambling onto the back of the black sea horse. Narissa recognized her at once. It was Tempestua, the girl who had been so rude when she arrived!

How dare she push me like that! thought Narissa. Then she stopped herself. There was no point in getting angry. *Forget it. Find another one*, she breathed to herself, and turned around to find a pretty pink-and-silver sea horse floating nearby. She read the name on his crest and saw that it was Moonshine.

"Hello, Moonshine," she greeted him, and a

little nervously, she held out the palm of her hand for him to sniff. His Sea Rider smiled, and swam away, leaving her alone with him.

As Moonshine nuzzled her fingers, Narissa patted his neck and eyed him up, trying to figure out how to mount. She grabbed ahold of his front fin and levered herself up so she could swing a leg over his back, then settled herself between the angular spines. She rested her hands on the top of the spine in front of her, thinking fast. What should she do now? How did she make him go forward? Some of the others had already started gliding around the arena. She didn't want to get left behind!

Instinctively, Narissa did what she did on Silver. With a quick stroke of her right hand and a gentle nudge with her left heel, she asked Moonshine to turn toward the right. He shifted, and Narissa gasped at the sudden movement, terrified she'd fall off. But then she realized she felt quite secure—and to her delight, the sea horse was doing what she asked. She nudged with both heels to speed him up just a little bit, and he obeyed again, falling in behind a bright coral-red sea horse with a curly-haired boy on its back. Narissa could feel a huge grin spreading over her face. She was actually doing it! She was riding a sea horse!

"Stop your mounts!" Neptuna's voice rolled around the arena.

Narissa gripped the spine in front of her and squeezed slightly. Moonshine angled his fins backward, then fluttered them gently, keeping himself in one place. Narissa felt exhilarated. It had been wonderful, even though Moonshine hadn't been her first choice. She glanced around to see what had happened to Tempestua and the black sea horse, and spotted them on the other side of the arena.

"Whoa, Storm!" she heard Tempestua say in her high, haughty voice.

So his name was Storm. Narissa could barely tear her eyes away from him as Neptuna began to give the next set of instructions.

"You will now change sea horses," Neptuna announced, her seaweed cloak billowing around her. "You will mount and dismount three times, so I may observe your agility. Then you will proceed around the arena. Look carefully, and you will see tiger cowrie shells scattered among the sand. Your task is to reach down and collect five of them."

Narissa stroked Moonshine's neck, then swung her leg around to dismount. She balanced herself on his fin before sliding down to the arena floor.

"Thank you so much, Moonshine," she whispered, then immediately looked across at Storm. Her heart sank. Another candidate was already at his side, and preparing to mount. If she was eliminated at this stage, she'd never get the chance to ride him!

You won't be eliminated, she told herself fiercely.

You can't *be!* She swam forward to the coral-red sea horse just in front of her and gazed up into her soft brown eyes. The name woven into her crest read Starburst.

Narissa greeted her, then paused for a second, wondering if there was a better way to mount than the one she'd already discovered—reaching up for the fin with her foot, then passing her leg over. But she couldn't see any other way. Quickly, she swung herself up, settled herself lightly between the spines, then lowered herself back down again. She did it again, and found that she was slightly faster this time. Once more, and she almost felt as though she'd been mounting sea horses all her life. *I'm getting there*, she thought.

But then she noticed something, out of the corner of her eye. Neptuna was making her way around the candidates, watching them closely as they performed the task. Some were being told to dismount and leave the arena. One girl who passed her was crying.

Narissa's heart began to thump hard. Candidates were being eliminated already! She remounted and nudged Starburst forward, scanning the sand below for a glimpse of a tiger cowrie. She spotted one, and leaned forward to pick it up.

She couldn't reach. No way! She almost fell off, and had to right herself hurriedly. She would have to ride Starburst closer to the floor, but how? She remembered how she asked Silver to dive, and she leaned forward. To her relief, it worked. The sea horse dipped her head, and swam lower so she was almost skimming the sand. Narissa turned her, and they passed the cowrie shell a second time.

Narissa took her chance. Bending low, she reached down and scooped—and there it was! A perfect tiger cowrie shell sat in the palm of her hand, its eye winking up at her. She pocketed it with a burst of excitement and turned Starburst around again, hunting for the next one. She was concentrating so hard that she hardly noticed what was happening to the other candidates. It was only when she swept up her last cowrie from the sparkling sand that she looked up and gasped.

More than two-thirds of the candidates were gone. With so few of them left, the arena felt more enormous than ever, its marble stands and swaying seaweed walls towering above her. She circled slowly, checking to see who else was still there. She saw the curly-haired boy . . . and Coral! Narissa started to smile. But then she saw Tempestua, too, riding ever so slightly faster than everyone else.

"Everybody stop," Neptuna's voice thundered from the center of the arena. "The task is finished."

Finished—and she had survived. Narissa trembled with excitement. Had she really made it through to the next stage? She hardly dared believe it. She pulled Starburst to a halt, and sat still to listen.

"Well done!" Neptuna looked at them with her steely green-blue eyes, her white hair swirling around her shoulders. "There are just twenty of you left. You are the ones who have shown natural ability, the basic skills that we require of any Sea Rider. But many more of you will fall at the next hurdle, for your most challenging task is yet to come."

Narissa's stomach was doing somersaults. So she *had* made it through—but the trials weren't over yet . . .

"Outside the Academy lies a treacherous stretch of seabed," Neptuna informed them. "You will all cross it, racing against one another. Success cannot be achieved by chance. Only the very best of you will win."

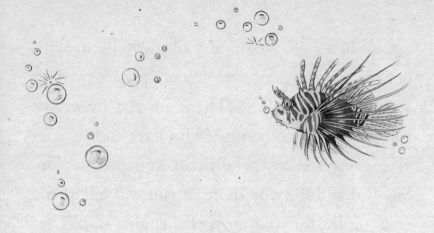

Chapter Four

"I WANT YOU all to swap sea horses again," Neptuna announced. "Then we will proceed to the racecourse."

Narissa had almost given up hope of ever riding Storm. The other competitors always seemed to get to him more quickly than she did. Everyone milled around, and Narissa scanned the arena for a free sea horse. Suddenly, to her delight, she realized that Storm had broken away from the others—and was swimming straight toward her!

Was it just coincidence, or had he actually picked her out? She didn't have time to think about it—Neptuna was already heading for the exit of the arena. Swiftly, Narissa mounted the beautiful black sea horse, and they all followed Neptuna outside. Now that she was finally on Storm's back, Narissa felt tingles all over. She was sure it was just excitement, but he seemed different than the other two sea horses she'd ridden.

Neptuna led them away from the city walls, and toward some huge jagged rocks that loomed up out of the ocean floor. As they drew closer, Narissa could see that they were dark and forbidding; even seaweed didn't seem to grow there very much. Neptuna came to a stop in their shadow, and turned to address the candidates.

"Ahead lies the Skeleton Crags," she announced. "They are full of treacherous gullies and deep crevices, deceptive currents and swirling whirlpools. It is exactly the sort of terrain that Sea Riders must enter to rescue creatures that are trapped or injured. However, there is a path through it—a challenging path, but one that you can clearly follow. This is the course for your race. Come. There is a starting line drawn in the sand."

Narissa gripped Storm's fin a little tighter. She was really nervous now, and she could feel her legs trembling. This was going to be so hard.

Don't worry. I'll keep you safe.

Narissa looked down at Storm. It was as if he had just spoken to her, not out loud, but in her head. She frowned. Had she imagined it? Whether she'd imagined it or not, her nerves seemed to have vanished, just like that. Instead, she felt calm and quietly confident as they all inched forward to the starting line.

We're going to be a great team, me and Storm, she thought to herself, and felt a thrill of excitement.

Neptuna raised her staff. "This race will test

your speed, agility, and, above all, your courage," she cried. "Candidates, are you ready?"

There was a brief pause as everyone shuffled forward and backward. Then came a brilliant flash through the water as Neptuna lowered her staff.

"Go!" she bellowed.

With a firm nudge from Narissa's heels, Storm surged forward. Narissa felt the water streaming past her as they plunged between the towering rocks, following a dark and winding alley as it snaked through the sea. Down, down, down they went, into the depths of a swirling chasm. They glided along it, twisting this way and that until suddenly, a wall of solid rock lay in their path, towering over them. Narissa gasped. She scanned the wall, looked up, and spotted a gap. She squeezed Storm's fin, and they rose rapidly, then plunged through the gap. It led to a long gully, and Storm leaped forward once more.

A Sea Rider race steward called out as they

passed. "Keep going! You've completed a third of the race!"

The gully was wide and flat, so Narissa risked a glimpse around her. The huge rock behind them had hidden many of the other racers from view, and she could see only three sea horses ahead of her.

"We're doing okay, Storm!" She inhaled, and shifted her weight farther forward up his neck so he could go even faster.

The sea horse raced on. They were going so fast that Narissa had to squint her eyes against the force of the water. The gully widened out, and she saw that they were gaining on the sea horse in front of them—it was Moonshine, the one she'd ridden first! Narissa pushed Storm forward, and her heart leaped as he made a huge effort, surging past Moonshine and his rider. Now only two other riders were ahead of them!

They bounded on, through a swirling pool that buffeted them from left to right, and then up over mounds of rocks that formed obstacles in their path. A deep-blue sea horse was leading the way, followed by a red-and-silver sea horse, and Narissa realized they were gaining on them. Then she recognized one of the riders—it was the friendly curly-haired boy she'd seen in the arena.

"We'll overtake him soon, I know we will!" said Narissa. For the briefest second, a thought flashed through her mind: *We're going to win!* But then she pushed it away. She had to concentrate! The curly-haired boy and his mount had disappeared through a crevice, and she steered Storm toward it.

"Careful, Storm," she muttered. "It's really narrow!"

They were just about to dive through when another sea horse came up alongside them. Narissa glanced sideways and caught a blur of blue and green, then yellow streaming hair. *Tempestua!* she thought.

They were almost at the crevice.

"Oh, no!" cried Narissa. There wasn't room for

both sea horses—and they were going too fast to stop! Narissa felt something smack into her side, knocking her clean off Storm's back. And then she was falling . . . falling . . . falling, deep into the crevice itself.

"Help . . . *Help!*" she cried.

High above, she saw Tempestua's face peering over her sea horse's shoulder. But then she'd gone, and Narissa was spinning through the water, upside down. Powerful currents swept her into an enclosed cavern. At last, she landed on the seabed with a bump.

It was dark. Narissa flexed her arms and legs one by one to check that she wasn't injured. Then she groped around in the darkness and peered up, hoping to see the light of the sun glimmering on the waves above. But she had fallen too far into the cavern—she could hardly see anything at all! Panic rose inside her. If she went the wrong way she could end up lost, deep in underwater caves . . . Thoughts of ferocious sea monsters filled her head.

It's all right, Narissa. I'm here.

Narissa stayed still. Had she imagined it? It wasn't exactly a voice. Just a feeling.

I'm right by your side.

She felt something nuzzle her. She reached out and touched Storm's strong neck. Then Narissa flung her arms around him. He'd

found her! She was so relieved she almost wanted to cry. But she couldn't do that. They had to get out of the cavern, and get to the end of the race.

"Oh, Storm. You saved me. You saved me!" she whispered, climbing onto his back. "Thank you!"

Leaning low over his back, Narissa rode Storm along the bottom of the cavern. Lifting one hand, she felt along the rocks above, searching for an opening. At last, the space seemed to open out up to the left.

"This way, Storm!" she exclaimed, nudging him in the right direction.

As the sea horse moved into the open space, Narissa saw light beaming down toward them through the crevice, and she gasped with joy.

"We're out again! Oh, Storm! We're safe!" she cried as he rose powerfully up through the black, pointed rocks of the crevice.

Narissa looked around her, searching for the way back onto the racecourse. But then, just as she spotted it, a Sea Rider approached them riding an elegant pearly sea horse.

"Stop there a minute!" he called. "I'm one of the race stewards. I saw how well you worked together to escape. Well done. I thought we would have to come and rescue you. It's rare to see teamwork like that before training has even begun."

His words made Narissa feel giddy with happiness. "Thank you," she said.

The steward smiled. "Now, keep going," he said. "You should at least finish the course."

Narissa stroked Storm's neck as they set off again. They were close to the finish line, but everyone else must have passed them by now. Narissa knew without looking back that they were last. All of her happiness faded away. However well she and Storm had worked together, they'd lost the race. She'd never be a Sea Rider now.

The candidates milled around, waiting for Neptuna to make her announcement. Many of them looked sad, knowing that they hadn't come close to being in the first four. But Narissa could hear someone who obviously felt differently. Tempestua!

"Of course, I knew I would qualify," she was telling someone in a loud voice.

Narissa decided to ignore her. She was trying not to think about the race or about what had happened. Instead, she concentrated on Storm, savoring every minute that she had left on his back. She would never get the chance to ride him again, and the thought filled her with sadness.

With her magnificent cloak billowing behind her, Neptuna suddenly appeared on a ledge in the rocks above them. Everyone gazed up at her as she raised her conch-shell staff.

"Candidates!" she boomed. "Form a line in front of me, please!"

With a little jostling, everyone hurried to obey her. Then Neptuna began to speak.

"This year, you all completed the race," she said. "For that, I must congratulate you. In other years, there have been candidates in need of rescue, and some who have lost their way. As you know, most of you will go home today and will not return. But I hope you will treasure the memory of riding our precious sea horses forever."

Narissa could feel tears pricking her eyes, and she bit her lip. Yes, she would always remember this day. She gripped Storm's silvery spine. Above all, she would always remember him.

"And now, the winners!" boomed Neptuna. "In first place, we have Finn, riding Magus. Come forward, Finn!"

There was a burst of applause as a dark-haired boy rode out of the line on a bronze-and-silver sea horse. Narissa realized that she hadn't even seen him when they were racing, so he must have been very far ahead! Finn brought Magus to a halt in front of Neptuna.

"Well done," she told him. "You showed exceptional skill today, Finn. Welcome to the Academy."

Finn bowed as his fellow candidates clapped again.

"Now, in second and third place we have Coral on Indigo, and Kelp on Firefly."

Narissa's heart gave a leap. Coral! She hadn't realized her new friend had been riding the deep-blue sea horse. She felt so happy for Coral, and clapped loudly as she rode forward. Curly-haired Kelp was by Coral's side, on the red-and-silver sea horse that Narissa and Storm had come so close to overtaking.

That could have been me with Coral, thought Narissa, disappointment welling up inside her.

"And the fourth rider is Tempestua, riding Aqua," finished Neptuna.

Tempestua let out a noisy whoop of triumph,

and Narissa noticed that several of her fellow candidates looked a little bit shocked—it wasn't nice to gloat like that when everyone else was going home. But Tempestua didn't seem to care. She rode forward with a broad, confident smile, and took her place alongside Kelp.

Narissa stared hard at Tempestua, thinking back to their clash during the race. She remembered calling out, and seeing the other girl's face high above her in the water. Hadn't Tempestua seen her? Had she really ignored Narissa, and ridden on, knowing that she was in danger? Surely not. No one who really understood what it meant to be a Sea Rider could have done such a thing. Narissa sighed heavily. Well, whatever had happened, there was no point in thinking about it now. Tempestua was going to the Academy. Narissa wasn't, and that was that.

I will miss you.

Narissa started, but she knew exactly where the

words were coming from. She placed her hand on Storm's neck. "I'll miss you, too, Storm," she whispered.

Now that the Academy places had been announced, she expected Neptuna to start dismissing everyone, but the great Sea Rider raised her staff one last time.

"These are our four winners. They have earned their place at the Academy with their speed and agility. But this year, I have something else to announce."

Another figure appeared on the rock ledge at Neptuna's side. Narissa frowned. She was sure she recognized him. Yes, it was the Sea Rider who had spoken to her when she and Storm had emerged from the cavern.

"Speed and agility are indeed essential for every Sea Rider," Neptuna continued. "But we require other qualities, too. And one of those is the ability to work well with your sea horse." She placed a hand on the shoulder of the Sea Rider. "One of the race stewards observed an exceptional piece of teamwork today when one of you got into trouble. And so, as a special exception, I am going to create a place at the Academy for that rider."

Narissa couldn't believe her ears. She hardly dared look at the steward. Was Neptuna really talking about *her*? She raised her eyes timidly and saw that the Sea Rider was gazing directly at her with a beaming smile on his face.

"Narissa and Storm, please come forward!" called Neptuna.

"Oh!" Narissa was so shocked she could hardly move. Her fellow candidates gave her a huge round of applause as she rode Storm forward to join the line of winners. It was incredible—after everything that had happened, they'd done it, after all.

"Well done, Narissa. You achieved something very special today," Neptuna told her.

Narissa couldn't stop smiling. She felt Storm prance beneath her. With a rush of delight, she realized he was dancing with joy!

Chapter Five

"Move up a bit, Crest!" said Narissa's dad. "Make sure there's room for all of us!"

Crest wriggled forward on Silver the dolphin's back. "If I go any farther, I'll be sitting on his head!" he giggled.

"You're all right, sweetheart," said his mom. "Hold tight, I'm coming up behind you."

Narissa's mom mounted Silver behind Crest, and Narissa climbed up next. Her dad got on last, riding in the most difficult place—back near the dolphin's tail, with Narissa's barnacle suitcase balanced on his knees.

"And we're off!" he exclaimed. "Give Silver a nudge, Narissa. You're the Sea Rider, after all."

Narissa laughed. "Not yet, Dad!" she said. "I'm only a trainee!"

But she did as he said and urged the dolphin forward. Silver turned in a lazy circle, then headed in the direction of Pearl Reef. With the whole family on board, he could only swim very slowly—it was so different from riding Storm. But Narissa didn't mind. It was her first day of training at the Academy, and she was thrilled that her whole family was coming to drop her off.

Her mom spent the entire journey giving Narissa advice. "Make sure you're always polite," she said. "I've heard that Neptuna's very strict, but she's also very fair, so make sure you do what she says."

"I will," Narissa promised.

"We're very proud of you," her mom continued. "Never forget that. Your training won't be easy, Narissa. But whenever things get difficult, remember that we're all here to support you."

"I know. Thanks, Mom."

"And above all, try to stay safe," said her mom. "I know it's a huge honor to train as a Sea Rider, but the work can be very dangerous. Please be careful, and don't take too many risks."

Narissa nodded, and drew a deep breath. Pearl Reef was in sight now, and her new life was about to start. Silver swam at a steady, easy pace until they reached the great Academy gates. She slid down from his back, and her dad handed her the little suitcase.

"Take care, Narissa," chorused her family. "We'll miss you!"

As Silver turned to head back home, they all waved and blew kisses. Crest made faces as usual, making Narissa laugh. She waved back and watched them until they were out of sight.

This is it! she said to herself, and, clutching her barnacle suitcase, she swam up to the gates.

Inside, a Sea Rider was waiting for her.

"Hi, I'm Narissa," the young sea nymph said shyly.

"Welcome, Narissa," the woman replied. "My name's Serenia. We've been expecting you. Follow me."

They swam along the elegant marble corridors lined with sea oak doors, and Narissa was soon feeling lost. The Academy was much bigger than she'd realized! She gazed up at the thousands of twinkling lantern fish above them, and felt like pinching herself. Was she *really* here?

Eventually, Serenia opened a door, and ushered Narissa inside.

"This is your dormitory," she explained. "You'll

be sharing with the two other trainee girls. Go on in—you have a little time to yourself now, to make yourself at home. I'll be back soon."

"Thank you," said Narissa shyly.

But as she entered the room her heart sank. The first thing she saw was Tempestua. She was busy hanging a seashell mosaic above her bed, so she didn't notice Narissa come in. Narissa looked around. The room was circular and quite simple, but it was carved out of the same white marble as the rest of the building, which glistened in the light from the lantern fish. The three beds were arranged around the curve of the room, with alcoves cut out of the marble where they could place their belongings. Narissa saw that Tempestua had snagged the bed with the biggest set of alcoves, and spread her things all over the little rock table that sat in the middle of the room. There were flowing sea silk dresses, necklaces of rare coral, and belts encrusted with rich sea minerals. Narissa stared at them all in disbelief. They had come here to work and train really hard. When did Tempestua think she was going to wear all of that?

But then she pushed the thoughts away. Perhaps Tempestua would be nicer now that they were all trainees together.

"Hi, Tempestua," she said.

Tempestua spun around. "Oh. It's you," she said. "Oh, well. I guess you won't be here for long."

Narissa was baffled. "Why?"

Tempestua stepped away from the mosaic, and jumped down from her bed. "Well, you didn't really win your place, did you? You'll probably be sent home soon."

"What's that supposed to mean?" Narissa's face flushed with anger. "If it weren't for you, Storm and I would have—" She stopped herself. She didn't want to lose her temper. One thing was very clear: Tempestua hadn't changed a bit.

"You and Storm would have what?" continued

Tempestua in a mocking tone. "As I remember, you fell off your sea horse. Not the kind of thing that *real* Sea Riders do very often!"

Narissa decided to ignore her. She swam over to the bed that was farthest away from Tempestua's and placed her barnacle suitcase on top of it. It looked very old and battered compared to her roommate's expensive things, but it had belonged to her mom when she was younger, and Narissa loved it. She opened it and began to take out her belongings—a few trinkets to remind her of home, her grandmother's dress for special occasions, three of her simple seaweed dresses, two pretty necklaces, and some oyster-shell bangles. That was all.

The bed was made from strips of giant palm grass woven together to form a springy mattress, with a soft blanket of sea puff cotton laid on top. Narissa placed her things carefully in the alcove behind it, and then she spotted something else—a uniform, laid out on the bed, ready for her to wear! It was a little bit like the one that they had worn for the trials: most of it was silvery-gray; but instead of plain turquoise bands around the waist and down the legs, there were rich emerald and ruby ones, with patterns embroidered in silver over the top.

"How lovely," whispered Narissa. She held it up to see it better.

"Ooh! Is that our new uniform?" exclaimed a voice.

Narissa spun around in delight. "Coral!" she cried. "You're here!"

"Yes, I'm a little late," said Coral. "We got caught in a school of snooper fish on the way here. I guess this one is mine." She put her bag down on the third bed and smiled at Tempestua. "Hi, Tempestua. Looks like you got here first!"

Tempestua gave a brief smile and nodded. "It's best to arrive early when you have a lot to unpack,"

she said, and began to fold one of her beautiful dresses.

Coral giggled. "It's a good thing I don't, then!" she said. "Serenia told me we should put on our uniforms. She'll be coming to take us to Neptuna's office soon."

"Oh, good," said Narissa. "I was dying to try it on anyway!"

Quickly, the three girls slipped into the cute outfits. Narissa was amazed to find that hers was a perfect fit . . . and really comfortable, too. She was already feeling a lot happier now that Coral had arrived. She felt sure that they'd become friends, and that would make it a lot easier to cope with Tempestua.

There was a knock at the door and Serenia peered around it.

"Ready, girls?" she called. "Neptuna's waiting for you."

They followed Serenia to a majestic domed

chamber lined with thousands of pearly pyramid shells. Neptuna sat holding her staff, in a chair decorated with golden sea twine. It was so magnificent it looked like a throne.

"Welcome!" Neptuna greeted them. "Come and sit here with the boys."

Just to one side of her throne sat Finn and Kelp on two stools made of driftwood. Serenia fetched three more from an alcove, then quietly disappeared as the girls sat down in a row.

"Now, before you do anything at all, I'd like you to learn a little of the Academy's history," said Neptuna. "Many years ago, there were no Sea Riders, and no one to patrol the ocean. And Oceana faced many problems. The number of pirate fish were getting out of control; there were more lionfish attacks out on the reefs; and on top of that, this was a time of dangerous tides that cast many creatures into danger."

Neptuna paused to sweep back her long white

hair. "It was my great-great-grandmother Galantea who first tamed wild sea horses," she carried on. "She learned that by working together, we could all be a force for good. She tamed the great golden sea horse, Titani, and became the first Sea Rider. Then she began to train others. And that is how the Academy began."

Narissa listened, spellbound. She had heard of Galantea, but she hadn't known that Neptuna was her great-great-granddaughter! And she hadn't known about Titani, either. She thought of Storm, and wondered if Galantea had understood Titani in the same way.

"Since that time, the role of the Sea Riders has become more and more important," said Neptuna. "The ocean is wonderful, but it is also full of peril. It is our job to seek information about what is happening in the deepest corners of Oceana. We must rescue any creature in difficulty, patrol for hidden dangers, and protect our world from threats."

Neptuna looked at them one by one, fixing them with her flashing blue-green eyes. "If you pass your testing period and complete your full training, that will become your job, too."

Narissa gazed back at her, feeling very serious. So there was still a test to pass. She thought of Tempestua's words: *I guess you won't be here for long*. She took a deep breath, and remembered riding Storm. She couldn't let Tempestua knock her confidence. She would just have to prove her wrong.

Neptuna got to her feet, her seaweed cloak swirling around her. "And now," she said, "it's time for you to meet the sea horses."

Chapter Six

NEPTUNA LED THE trainees out of her office and through the halls, then stopped at a narrow door in the main wall of the Academy. She held it open for the five trainees. They swam through, and found themselves in a beautiful sea meadow that stretched out beyond the walls of the city and to the sea beyond.

"Wow!" cried Narissa and Coral, both at the same time.

Waving sea grasses grew right across the meadow, some quite fine and short, others reaching up for the sunlight that glinted above their heads. The sea horses grazed among them, their brilliant colors blending in with the vibrant shades of the grass. Narissa noticed Firefly, the lovely red-and-silver sea horse that Kelp had ridden in the race. There was a pretty amber sea horse at his side, covered in gold spots that started big and bold on her back, then became tiny little dots on her belly.

"Follow me," said Neptuna, and set off around the edge of the meadow.

Narissa couldn't stop gazing at the sea horses. They looked so tranquil here, feeding among the sea grasses. In a separate little paddock, she spotted a baby with his tail entwined around his mom's, both the same bright pink with softer, pale pink stripes.

Then her heart stopped. "Storm!"

The huge black sea horse had spotted the sea

nymphs coming, and stopped grazing. Narissa looked at him longingly. Would he recognize her, she wondered? He seemed to be looking straight at her. Then he gave a trilling whinny, and Narissa felt a jolt of excitement. She was sure it was just for her!

Neptuna stopped and turned to address them. "This is the main meadow," she explained. "It's where the sea horses can relax and graze. Most of them will come when called, especially to their own Sea Rider. Others might need tempting with a little treat."

Some of the sea horses were starting to drift over, anxious to greet their leader. A feisty youngster swam up to Neptuna and butted her playfully on the arm.

"Ah! Alecto," chuckled Neptuna. "Always up to your tricks." She stroked his neck and then his fine, eager face. "You're one of my trainee sea horses, aren't you? And soon you'll be ready for work."

Alecto snorted, his big nostrils flaring. The little group of sea horses drew closer. Storm floated in the middle of them, bigger than any of the others.

"You may approach them," Neptuna told the trainees. "But be careful not to startle them."

Immediately, Tempestua pushed Narissa to one side, and swam straight up to Storm. "Can I have this one?" she demanded.

Narissa's heart beat faster. If Tempestua nabbed Storm right from the beginning, it would break her heart!

But she shouldn't have worried. "You won't be given any one sea horse in particular," Neptuna told her. "You will ride many different ones as part of your training. It's an essential part of the process."

Tempestua stuck her bottom lip out. "But I thought every Sea Rider had their own special horse," she said sulkily.

"Yes, eventually," said Neptuna. "But only when

you match."

"What does *matching* mean?" asked Coral.

"Ah," Neptuna said with a smile. "Matching is one of the most magical things about being a Sea Rider."

Narissa noticed that a tall, slender sea horse of shimmering greenish-blue had joined the group. Now she swam silently over to Neptuna and bent her head over the sea nymph's shoulder. She had huge dark eyes that sparkled trustingly as Neptuna reached up to stroke her.

"This is Talassa," she said. "She is my match. Matching is something ancient and very mystical. Galantea believed that it existed long before she founded the Academy—that it was a deep secret known only to a few sea nymphs. It happens when a sea nymph and a sea horse discover a special bond, one that is based on temperament and skills—and also magic."

Narissa couldn't take her eyes off Storm. She

thought of the strange way that they had under-stood each other during the race. She thought of how she had felt his voice, speaking somewhere inside her. Could it be possible that he was her match?

"Finding your match can take many years," continued Neptuna. "It generally happens only once a Sea Rider's training is complete. Even then, it is not at all automatic. So, trainees, don't concern yourselves with matching for now. It is more important for you to develop your skills."

Narissa sighed and swallowed her disappointment. She would have to forget the idea. Maybe it was just that Storm was special, and anyone who rode him felt the same things. No wonder Tempestua wanted to pick him all the time!

"And now, before you start riding, I want you to meet Caspian," said Neptuna.

From between some clumps of blue-gray sea

grass, another Sea Rider appeared. Narissa recognized him at once—he was the steward they had met during the race! She would never forget what he had done. If he hadn't reported to Neptuna about her escape with Storm, Narissa wouldn't be at the Academy at all. She would feel grateful to him forever.

He came and stood alongside Neptuna, and Narissa saw that he was older than she remembered. His short hair was silvery-gray, matching his mother-of-pearl uniform, but he was still athletic and strong, with piercing wisdom in his grayish-blue eyes. He was even taller than Neptuna, and a good deal broader, too.

"Caspian will be your mentor during your training," Neptuna told them. "He will organize your schedule day by day, teaching you riding skills and all the necessary Sea Rider secrets. He will assess your progress and correct you when you make a mistake. And if any of you have problems or difficulties, you should turn to Caspian for advice."

Narissa felt thrilled. It would be wonderful to work with such a just and fair-minded teacher. She listened eagerly as Caspian stepped forward and began to speak.

"We will get started shortly," he said in his deep, powerful voice. "I am going to choose five sea horses for you to ride today. Wait here while I gather them together."

He glided smoothly toward the herd and began to make his selection. Narissa watched as he picked out Aqua, Tempestua's sea horse in the race; Starburst, the lovely coral-red female that Narissa had ridden to collect cowries in the arena; Orion, a striking male with a purple body and pure white crest and fins; Magus, Finn's bronze-and-silver winning mount and then, to Narissa's delight, he picked Storm.

Caspian swam around the other sea horses with his arms outstretched, encouraging them to return to their grazing. Then he turned to the trainees.

"Here are your five sea horses," he said. "I'd like you to choose one of them and mount."

Eagerly, Narissa turned toward Storm—but she saw at once that Tempestua had beaten her to it. *Oh, that girl!* she thought in exasperation. But then she shrugged. Her turn would come—Caspian would make sure that their training was carried out fairly. She decided to try a new mount and headed for Orion.

"Hello, boy," she murmured, and swung herself up between his spines. Orion was fine-boned and energetic, and Narissa could tell at once that he would be an exciting ride, responding to the slightest nudge from her heels. She grinned to herself. Yes, she loved Storm most of all, but riding *any* of the sea horses felt amazing!

"Today, we will just go for a brief ride, so I can observe your riding skills," Caspian told them. He whistled, and his own pearly sea horse appeared from a far corner of the meadow. He mounted, and beckoned to the trainees. "Follow me," he said, and they set off, winding their way through the sea grass.

Chapter Seven

THE NEXT MORNING, Serenia picked up the girls to take them to breakfast. She led them into a big hall that was open to the ocean above, the morning sun lighting up the rows of stone benches. The boys were already there, digging into a feast— plump seaweed cakes, crab cakes, sea apples and pears, and many different kinds of seaweed pancakes.

"I hope there's crackle sea bread," said Tempestua. "That's what we have at home."

"I'm afraid not," said Serenia with a smile. "It's a little expensive."

"I'd have thought the Academy could afford it," said Tempestua haughtily.

"Well, I'm sure you'll find something you can enjoy," said Serenia. She turned away from Tempestua and spoke to the others. "When you're finished, I'll take you to the grooming area. This morning you're going to learn how to groom the sea horses."

"Thank you, Serenia," Narissa and Coral said in unison as the Sea Rider glided away.

Narissa sat down next to Finn. She'd been fascinated by him ever since he'd won the race—he was so quiet, but she could feel he had lots of energy just beneath the surface. She reached for a pancake and smiled at him.

"Had you really never ridden a sea horse before the trials?" she asked him.

Finn shook his head. "No. But I grew up riding

great barracudas," he admitted. "It's really good practice."

Narissa's eyes widened. Riding great barracudas was a dangerous sport, and very few sea nymphs took part in it. Many of those who did ended up with nasty injuries.

"Will you keep doing it, now you're here?" she asked.

"No. I'd rather be a Sea Rider," said Finn. "Riding great barracudas is just a hobby. My brother almost died in a great-barracuda race last year."

"I'm so sorry," said Narissa. No wonder Finn seemed so serious.

Just then, Kelp interrupted them. "Narissa, can you pass me those sea pears?" he asked. "I think Coral would like to try them!"

Coral looked astonished. "How do you know?"

Kelp blushed. "I noticed you looking at them," he confessed.

Narissa caught Coral's eye, and they grinned

at each other. Ever since they'd been to the sea meadow the day before, Kelp hadn't stopped trying to help Coral. Narissa was sure he really liked Coral, and she wasn't surprised—with her bouncy black curls and warm, friendly face, Coral was lovely!

When Serenia returned to take them to the grooming area, they climbed a staircase that wound toward the surface of the sea, and then opened out onto a marble platform that was bright from the light of the sun. Some of the marble had been polished so it reflected even more light, dazzling the whole area.

"We came from inside the Academy, but you can swim directly up here on a sea horse," Serenia explained. "There's a path from the meadow."

Caspian was waiting for them with the five sea horses that they'd ridden the day before—plus Moonshine and Indigo—and he explained what they needed to do.

"A sea horse has a delicate crest and fins," he told them. "But there are many tiny seashells and fish that try to latch onto them. Some of them are so tiny that they're difficult to see, and that's why we groom up here near the surface. We need the bright light of the sun to do the job correctly."

He showed them a box containing sea sponges and combs, then picked up a sea sponge and began

to work on Orion. "Any sea horse with white fins and crest, like Orion, is easy to groom," he said. "When their fins are clean, you can almost see through them. With the others, you must be very careful to clean them properly, but don't rub too hard. Sea horses will let you know if you're hurting them! Now, take a sponge and get to work."

Tempestua stepped in front of Coral and grabbed a sponge. "I'm grooming Storm," she announced, before anyone else could make a choice.

Narissa sighed and got to work on Moonshine instead. Kelp dove into the box and found a sponge that was almost new.

"Coral, look!" he exclaimed. "Here. You can have this one."

"Thanks, Kelp," said Coral. "That's really nice of you."

This time, Narissa avoided catching her friend's eye. If she did, she was sure she would giggle. Instead, she concentrated on Moonshine. He seemed a bit ticklish, and jumped skittishly as she cleaned the fins lower down his back. She stroked his neck for a while, soothing him, and he began to calm down. Then she worked steadily, cleaning his fins and crest first on one side, then shifting him around so his other side was in the sun. Out of the corner of her eye, she watched Finn. He was grooming Firefly without talking to anyone. He did everything so quickly and gently, without any fuss, but he must have been really brave to ride those great barracudas. No wonder he won the race!

When they'd finished with the sponges, Caspian showed them how to use a sea comb to tidy the crests at the top of the sea horses' heads. Then he told them to gather around him.

"Today, you're going to do an important exercise," he said. "An essential part of being a Sea

Rider is working as a team. It's the only safe way to carry out many of the rescues that we need to do. So I am going to take you to an old deserted castle outside of Pearl Reef. There will be a Sea Rider hiding somewhere, and your job will be to work together to find him."

Narissa felt a quiver of excitement. What a cool assignment!

"This time, I'm going to decide which sea horses you should ride," Caspian carried on. "Tempestua, you're on Moonshine. Kelp, take Aqua. And, Coral, take Orion. Finn, I'd like you to ride Starburst."

Narissa was holding her breath. There were only Firefly, Magus, and Storm left. *Please, Caspian*, she silently begged.

"And Narissa, you're riding Storm," Caspian finished.

Narissa's face split into a grin. She swam over to Storm and stroked his wise, handsome face, then patted him on the neck before mounting. It felt wonderful to climb onto his shining black back again. He was so big and strong compared to the others, yet Narissa felt completely at home riding him. They followed Caspian out of the Academy and along the streets of Pearl Reef. Narissa felt a flush of pride as angelfish and messenger eels darted out of their way, showing their respect for the sea horses. Then they passed through the city gates and headed down into a deep ocean valley, where Narissa could just see the turrets of an old castle in the turquoise water. It seemed colder here, and she shivered as they approached. The castle must have been splendid once, with its high walls and spires covered in shiny pink shells; but now wild clumps of straggly blue seaweed crept through its stones, and most of the shells were gone.

They stopped outside a dark, gaping entrance. There had once been a gate, but now there were just crumbling columns on either side of the black hole, with hermit crabs living in their hollows.

"This is where you'll start your mission," Caspian told them. "You must all go inside and work as a team to figure out the best way to find the hidden Sea Rider. Meet me here when you have succeeded."

Moonshine and Aqua seemed to hesitate, pulling away from the gate, while Tempestua and Kelp tried to turn them around.

"I don't mind leading us in," offered Finn.

He turned Starburst toward the gloomy entrance and gently urged her inside. The sea horse reared up a little, showing her fear, but then she did as Finn said. Narissa was impressed—Finn seemed to know how to get the best out of a sea horse already. Feeling reassured, the other sea horses followed him, and they all found themselves in a huge, ancient hallway that was so dark Narissa could barely see. As her eyes adjusted, two sharp-toothed dogfish sharks darted by, their eyes cold and hungry, and Narissa caught sight of an enormous octopus, its tentacles groping across the floor.

It was the sort of place that Narissa's parents had always warned her to avoid. All sorts of dangerous sea creatures could be lurking here! She didn't like it one bit, but she'd have to forget that to do the assignment. She gripped Storm's spine nervously, and suddenly, that strange feeling came back . . .

Don't be afraid. I know this place very well.

It was such a relief to sense Storm's words again. Narissa felt instantly comforted and followed the others deeper into the chamber. All around them were broken-down columns and archways, smothered in green, slimy algae. Several stairways led up to other floors, just visible in the shadows above them.

"I think we should work in pairs," announced Tempestua. "A pair on each floor. That'd be the quickest way to find the Sea Rider, wouldn't it? If we all stay together, it'll take forever."

"*Hmm*, that makes sense," said Kelp.

"But there are five of us," said Coral. "That makes a two and a three."

"Yes, but Narissa has a really big sea horse," Tempestua pointed out. "She'll be all right on her own with Storm. Won't you, Narissa?"

Narissa was shocked. Tempestua wouldn't want to work on her own in a creepy castle like this, she was sure of it. But she knew exactly what Tempestua was doing. She was trying make Narissa's life as difficult as possible, so she'd fail the assignment. But Narissa had to say yes. If she said no, everyone would think she was a coward.

"I don't mind working alone," said Finn quietly. "Narissa can work with Coral."

Narissa hesitated, but then she heard Storm's voice again.

Say yes. You'll be safe with me.

Narissa's heart leaped. She placed a hand on Storm's neck, and shook her head. "It's okay, Finn," she said. "Tempestua's right. Storm *is* bigger than the other sea horses. I'm sure we'll be fine." She looked across at Tempestua with a cold smile. "I actually think it's a very good idea, actually. I'll search the first floor."

Tempestua looked surprised, then swung Moonshine away. "Good," she snapped. "Kelp, are you coming with me?"

Kelp looked helplessly at Coral, then shrugged and followed Tempestua.

Coral threw Narissa a sympathetic glance. "Will you be okay?" she whispered.

"Yes, I'll be fine," nodded Narissa. She would show Tempestua what she and Storm were made of! "You go with Finn."

"If you're sure." Coral smiled, then joined Finn at the bottom of a twisting staircase.

The others disappeared. Narissa was left on her own on Storm. Chilly currents swirled all around them.

Chapter Eight

IN SPITE OF what she'd said to Tempestua, Narissa's nerves started to get the better of her. She couldn't help it. A monstrous octopus was creeping in their direction, waving its ugly suckers in the water, and there was some other creature lurking in one of the corners. She couldn't see what it was, but it had a pair of red, bulbous eyes that were staring out at them.

"I don't like it here, Storm," she whispered.

There is nothing to be afraid of.

"All right. I'll try to believe you." Narissa held on tightly to Storm's spine, feeling a little bit better. Nudging him with her heels, she asked him to move forward, skirting around the octopus and toward one of the crumbling archways. Suddenly, a dagger eel with enormous pale eyes zoomed from a crevice, dive-bombing them, and Narissa ducked.

"Oh!" she gasped. "Storm, you said there was nothing to be afraid of!"

It cannot harm you.

The sea horse arched his neck and puffed out his chest, holding his ground against the eel while Narissa gripped his spine anxiously. The eel's eyes glittered, staring at them. But then, after a few seconds, it slithered off into the darkness, and Narissa let out a long, slow breath.

They continued through one archway, and then another. Narissa had almost forgotten that they were supposed to be looking for a Sea Rider, but now she started to hunt, peering through curtains of gray seaweed or behind great slabs of fallen stone. Nothing. They went on into a chamber that looked as though it may have been a bedroom— maybe even a young nymph's room. Narissa found a fragment of broken coral necklace and a shell trinket box with no lid. But no Sea Rider.

"Let's try the other side of the main chamber, Storm," she said, and guided him back out through the maze of archways. She thought she had remembered the way, but suddenly there was a mound of crumbled rock in front of them. It completely blocked their path, and Narissa stared at it in panic. Had part of the castle collapsed while they were there?

"Oh, Storm, are we trapped?" She gasped.

No. We can still go back. I remember how we came in.

Narissa turned the sea horse and realized she had missed the last arch that they had come through. With a sigh of relief, she turned Storm into the main chamber once more. As they crossed it and entered a different set of rooms, she began to relax. Storm was right. There really was nothing to be afraid of.

A school of tiny nibbler fish surrounded them as they explored a high room that might have been a study. Narissa batted them away, trying to peer through the darkness for the pearly silver of a Sea Rider's uniform. But then she heard a call from somewhere high above.

"Kelp! Narissa! We found him!"

It was Coral, her voice drifting down from the third floor.

Oh, good, thought Narissa. She was really happy for Coral and Finn. They both deserved to do really well as Sea Riders.

"We'll just have to do better next time," she whispered to Storm, stroking him.

She was about to turn him back into the main

chamber when she heard a strange noise. She listened carefully. Yes—there it was again! A whimper coming from the far end of the room.

"Do you hear that, Storm? It sounds like something in pain."

She swung him around and into the dark corner where the sound had come from. There was a tangle of dense, knotted seaweed, but underneath it, she could just make out the shape of a table. And then, beneath that, she caught a flash of orange.

Narissa heard the whimper again, and they dove in for a closer look.

"It's a sea dragon!" she exclaimed. "Look, Storm—it's a young one. And he's trapped!"

She slipped down from his back and parted the fronds of seaweed. The table was made of dark, heavy granite, but it had been sitting there for so long that it was encrusted with limpets and barnacles. The sea dragon whimpered again, then gave a squeak of fear as Narissa peered into his face. She was right—he was really young, with big dark eyes that looked terrified. His orange scales turned bright red as she examined him—a sure sign that he was truly frightened!

"Let's see what's happened to you," Narissa murmured soothingly. "Don't worry. I'm not going to hurt you."

She groped around under the table, pushing through the slippery seaweed, and discovered that one of his tentacles was caught under a table leg.

"How did you do that?" she asked, looking into the sea dragon's eyes. But he couldn't tell her. All he did was open his mouth again, and gave another squeak.

"Just stay calm. We'll get you free," said Narissa. She reached for the corner of the table and gave it a good heave. It didn't budge, not even a tiny bit. She tried again, hauling with all her strength. The sea dragon watched her with anxious eyes. He understood that she was trying to help him, she was sure. The trouble was, she simply couldn't!

She felt something butting her elbow, and found Storm there, touching her with his nose.

"Oh, Storm, what are we going to do?" she exclaimed.

To her surprise, Storm swam away from her, back along the murky room, then stopped and looked back to see if she had followed. Narissa caught up, feeling puzzled.

We can use this. It is very strong.

Narissa stared around her. What was Storm trying to tell her? He nosed a patch of giant sea twine, its twisty emerald fronds snaking right up toward the ceiling. Suddenly, Narissa understood. She loosened one of the twines from where it was anchored in a gap in the castle wall, and pulled it free. Then, together, they swam back to the little sea dragon.

Groping around in the darkness, Narissa tied

one end of the sea twine around the table leg. Her dad had taught her how to tie knots so they wouldn't come undone, but she did a double knot just in case. Then she turned to Storm and wrapped the other end around his long, spiraling tail. She knew that sea horses had amazingly strong tails—they could hold against the wildest seas! And Storm's was sure to be even stronger than most. He curled it around the sea twine and gripped it tightly.

Narissa clambered onto his back and took a deep breath. "We're ready," she told him, and squeezing the spine in front of her, she asked him to swim upward.

The mighty sea horse rose steadily. There was a jerk as the sea twine reached its full extent, and then Narissa could feel the strain all through Storm's body as he fluttered his fins furiously, tugging and tugging at the table. Slowly, slowly, she felt the heavy granite shift. Peering down over her shoulder, she saw the sea dragon suddenly wriggle

free in a cloud of bubbles.

With a squeal of joy, the little sea dragon swam up to join them, his eyes bright with gratitude.

Then Narissa heard Caspian's voice. "Narissa! Storm! Where are you?" he called from the main chamber.

He sounded worried, and Narissa realized they must have spent a lot of time rescuing the sea dragon. Everyone would be wondering what had happened to them. "Coming," she shouted back.

She slid down from Storm's back and swam to unwrap the sea twine from his tail. Then, as she mounted again, the baby sea dragon nuzzled up to her, and she took him into her arms.

"We're all safe now. Let's go!" she cried and urged Storm swiftly through the water.

Chapter Nine

CASPIAN WAS STANDING just inside the castle entrance, peering into the gloom with the other trainees gathered around him.

"Ah, Narissa, there you are!" he exclaimed, as Narissa and Storm swam up to them. "I was just about to start searching for you! Come on outside!"

They all swam out of the forbidding castle. Narissa breathed a sigh of relief. It was wonderful to be out in bright blue water again, with colorful fish floating in the sunlight above and no horrible sea monsters creeping up on her.

Then Caspian saw what Narissa was carrying. "What are you doing with a baby sea dragon?" he demanded.

"He was trapped," explained Narissa. "One of his tentacles was stuck under an old table. We had to use some sea twine to pull it up—I wrapped it around Storm's tail, and he managed to lift it. That's why we were late."

Caspian looked astonished. "You figured out how to do that with Storm?" he asked. "Well done! You carried out a genuine rescue, Narissa—that's very impressive!"

Narissa blushed. "Thank you. I'm a little worried, though," she said. "I don't know if the sea dragon's all right—did he hurt himself?"

"Let me see." Caspian dismounted and took the sea dragon from Narissa's arms.

The sea dragon wriggled and whimpered a little, his scales flashing from orange to red and back again as Caspian gently examined his injured tentacle.

"There's a little piece of barnacle shell caught in his flesh," said Caspian. "Do you see it here? I'm just going pull that out, then he'll be fine."

The sea dragon gave a loud squeal and went bright red as the Sea Rider gripped the piece of barnacle tightly and pulled it out. Then he slowly faded to orange as he realized that his pain had gone. Narissa reached and stroked his head, comforting him.

"There. He'll do just fine now," said Caspian. "Should we let him go?"

"How will he find his family?" asked Coral anxiously.

"You don't need to worry about that," Caspian told her. "Young sea dragons stray a long way from their families. I'm sure that's why Narissa found him on his own in the first place. They always find their way home again—they have a special instinct for it."

Coral looked relieved.

Caspian gave the sea dragon one last check all over, then let it go. It swam off joyfully, waving its six appendages and making chirpy squeaks. Caspian smiled. "So, we have plenty to report back to Neptuna," he said. "And let's not forget Coral and Finn, who found the hidden Sea Rider. She was hiding in a very dark and treacherous part of the castle, so well done to them. But Narissa and Storm are our Sea Rider heroes for today."

Everyone burst into a round of applause—everyone except Tempestua. Narissa caught a glimpse of her scowl and realized that she must be furious. She hadn't won the challenge, she hadn't been able to ride Storm, *and* Narissa had done better than her, despite her plotting to make Narissa fail.

But that was too bad. Coral, Kelp, and Finn were obviously really happy for Narissa, and that was all that mattered. As they set out for the Academy, they gathered around her as closely as they could.

"The sea dragon was so *cute*!" said Coral. "And really tiny, too! How did you find him?"

"Did Storm help you use the sea twine?" asked Kelp. "Did he just hold it with his tail, or did you tie it on?"

"How did you ask him to lift the stone?" Finn wanted to know.

Narissa laughed as they bombarded her with questions all at once. She patted Storm's neck, and explained how they'd found the baby sea dragon, where they'd found the sea twine, and how they'd used it to lift the table. "Storm's amazing," she said. "He knew exactly what to do. I couldn't have done any of it without his help!"

"Yes, but *you* were riding him," said Coral

warmly. "I'm not sure I could have done all those complicated things with the sea twine!"

Narissa hesitated. She hadn't told them *every* detail. She hadn't explained that Storm seemed to understand her—and speak to her, too. Should she tell them? she wondered. She thought quickly, and decided it would sound much too boastful

"Of course you would," she told Coral. "You'll see, when something like that happens to you."

They reached the Academy, happy and tired, and took the sea horses back to the meadow to rest. Before letting him go off to graze, Narissa threw her arms around Storm's neck to give him one last hug. Then Caspian called them to go and see Neptuna.

"I've given her my report," he said. "I think she's going to be very pleased with you all."

Narissa felt her excitement rising as they approached Neptuna's chamber once more. She felt so lucky to have made the rescue—and so happy that Caspian had let her ride Storm. Whatever Tempestua might say or do, she was sure she belonged at the Academy now.

"Welcome!" boomed Neptuna as they entered the chamber. "And congratulations! I've heard all about your achievements today." Her face, usually so stern, was wreathed in a sparkling smile. "Come here and let me look at you!"

The five of them followed Caspian to stand in front of her, and bowed their heads in respect.

"You have done exceptionally well today," Neptuna told them. "You worked well as a team to find the Sea Rider. And, of course, you made a genuine rescue, too."

Narissa glanced sideways at Tempestua's face, and saw that she was scowling again. Narissa sighed. It was such a shame that they couldn't be friends, but unless Tempestua changed, there was no chance of that.

"I am very proud of all of you," said Neptuna, "and I am happy to announce that you have all passed your testing period. You will continue your training as Sea Rider cadets." She paused and beckoned a Sea Rider who was standing a few paces behind her magnificent chair. "Please bring me those awards, Merion."

Coral and Narissa exchanged glances. Awards! What kind of awards? Narissa had never imagined anything so exciting. The Sea Rider went to an alcove to one side of the office and picked up a soft cushion made of fine sea silk. On top of it lay five mother-of-pearl bowls, twinkling with tiny jewels. Narissa gasped. They were amazing!

"These bowls are a special gift for those who excel during their assignment," said Neptuna. "They are yours to keep in your rooms. Narissa, please come forward."

Almost trembling with excitement, Narissa went to receive her bowl.

"Well done, Narissa," Neptuna praised her. "I'm particularly proud of you."

Narissa looked up into the Sea Rider's eyes. For once, they were soft and warm, and full of encouragement. "Thank you," she managed to whisper back.

She examined her bowl as the others received

theirs. It was so delicate, and all the jewels caught the light, flashing around the room. She had never owned anything so beautiful in her life before.

"Now you may rest for a while," said Neptuna. "But it is not often that a group of young cadets shows such promise. So this evening, as a reward, there will be a celebratory dinner. You will sample some of the finest food that Pearl Reef can offer— and I can assure you, that is *very* fine!"

"Thank you, Neptuna!" they all said in chorus.

Narissa couldn't stop smiling. She looked around at her new friends—Coral, Kelp, and Finn. Then she thought of Storm, and how amazing it had been to work with him inside the castle. Tempestua was still looking moody, but nothing could spoil how wonderful their first day had been. Life at the Academy was so special, and Narissa couldn't wait to see what tasks would lie ahead.

Look for Narissa's next adventure:

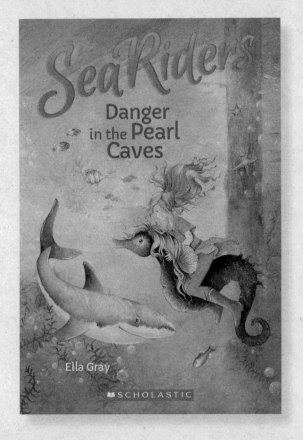

When the Sea Rider cadets travel to the dangerous Black Pearl Caves, anything can happen!